# My Little Corner of the World

## By

# Beth Burch Smith

ISBN 1-878096-36-2

**For additional copies of this book contact:**
**Texas Forestry Association**
**PO Box 1488**
**Lufkin TX 75902-1488**
**(409) 632-TREE**
**FAX (409) 632-9461**
Printed in Hong Kong

Dedicated to Tommy Smith.
I hope you always remember that God created everything
for a purpose.

And to my Dad.
Thank you for your love and support.
And for teaching me to look at both sides of an issue fairly.

I love you both.

My little corner of the world is filled with hundreds of things to do, but of all these things, my favorite thing to do is to walk and look at the tall green trees.

This morning I took a long walk down the clear running creek. I waded through the cold water and felt the silky sand rise between my toes. I looked up and down the creek and saw huge, gigantic trees towering over me with their branches shading the sandy banks.

I watched as squirrels leaped from branch to branch as if they had no care in the world. I listened to the birds singing and the woodpeckers pecking, watching quietly as the wildlife went about its daily routine.

Climbing up a steep bank, I made my way to the top. I looked across what seemed to be an empty and lifeless clearing. There were piles of debris left from a past timber harvest. Tears filled my eyes because the beauty of the tall pine trees was gone.

I felt a heavy hand bear down on my small shoulder. I turned around and placed my hand above my eyes to block out the rays of the sun. The tall man was staring straight down at me.

With tear filled eyes, I smiled at him. The tall man was my grandpa. He had cleared the land the year before. He knelt down beside me and wiped a tear from my cheek. I looked sadly at him and asked him why he did such an awful thing. He responded by telling me a long but educating story.

He began by telling me that trees are capable of doing many tasks. They use their roots to support the land, and to filter the water. They help supply the world with clean air, and some animals make their homes in the trees.

As my grandfather talked, my eyes caught the movement of a family of deer playing in the field below. When he noticed that my attention had strayed away from him, he pointed to the deer. "You see those deer?" he asked. "Those deer are taking advantage of this clear cut. You see, son, the clear cut has created a rebirth of new forest for the animals."

Cutting trees is not bad if you will follow a few, but very important steps. The key to cutting timber is replanting. Always remember that for every tree you cut, you must replant seven in its place. Trees are the world's only renewable resource. That's why it is important that we monitor the cutting and replanting of trees closely.

"The trees from this piece of land were taken to a mill where they were processed into lumber and paper. Your parents saved some of the timber and had it cut so that they could build your new house."

"I replanted this land with thousands of little pine seedlings, and in 18 years you can selectively cut some of the trees, and pay your way to college."

"If you follow these few rules, you can consider yourself an environmentalist. Keep these thoughts with you always so that you can educate others about the importance of timber harvesting."

You know, my Grandpa has told me many stories over the years, but none of them has meant as much as this one.

When my Grandpa walked away from me that day, I saw my little corner of the world in a new and brighter light.

## About the author...

Beth Smith, 24, a student at Stephen F. Austin State University in Nacogdoches, Texas, was working as a substitute teacher for the Brookeland schools at the time she wrote "My Little Corner of the World." The book is based on an experience by her son, Tommy, 4, the grandson of an East Texas harvesting contractor.

She had written the book just prior to Wednesday, August 10, 1994, when she was killed in an auto accident at Brookeland.

Beth is buried in the family cemetery in a forest near Brookeland. In addition to Tommy, Beth and her husband Todd had one other child, Tristin, 2. She was the daughter of Tommy and Velma Burch.

The book, published by the Texas Forestry Association, is made possible by donations in memory of Beth Burch Smith's lifelong love for the forests.

Beth Burch Smith walked into my university classroom with a burning determination to change the world one kid at a time. With her warm green eyes, her ready smile, and her inquisitive nature, she was a delight to her teachers and an inspiration to her peers. Her commitment to her parents, her husband, and her children set an example for other students who were juggling classes and families. Her Christian faith radiated to all those with whom she came in contact.

Although a tragic accident took Beth away from us; her vision to impact the lives of children will be perpetuated through the Beth Burch Smith Memorial TAIR Scholarship Program, established at Brookland ISD, and her book "My Little Corner of the World," written as a university student.

Reba Powers
Adjunct Professor
Department of Elementary Education
Stephen F. Austin State University